RIPLEY'S MISSING LOCKET

Written by
Connie Herrick

Illustrated by
Mark Herrick

ISBN Hardcover: 978-1-7376514-3-7
ISBN Paperback: 978-1-7376514-4-4
ISBN eBook: 978-1-7376514-5-1

Library of Congress Control Number: 2021925725

First hardcover edition 2022

DESIGN: PIPER MURAKAMI
COPY EDITOR: DOUGLAS JACKSON

RipleyandFriendz.com

With deep love for our incredible
son Matt, our search and rescue
wonder dogs Pele and Kapo, Hariel and
the fishies, and of course Ripley.

RIPLEY

Ripley admired herself in the mirror. Her new locket sparkled as she moved her head from side to side.

"I look incredible! Truly spectacular!" she exclaimed with a satisfied sigh.

"My new locket is fabulous. I look so important and smart. It's time to show my friends so they can admire my locket, and me of course."

Ripley continued to preen in front of the mirror, pretending to show off her new locket to a crowd of adoring fans.

"Hey, Catnip Collective! Check out my new locket!" squealed Ripley.

"It's puurrfection," meowed the Collective.

"Well, smelly sisters, what do you think of my amazing new locket?" asked Ripley.

"It's very shiny and very nice," said Pele. Kapo thought a new ball would be more exciting, but kept that thought to herself.

"Howdy, Nash! Look at my new locket! Isn't it pretty?" asked Ripley.

"Is it heavy? Will it make you run slower for Touch Nose Tag?" asked Nash hopefully.

"Hey, Mattie and Topher! Look at my new locket! Isn't it sparkly?" puffed Ripley.

"The sunlight bounces off it in the most delightful way," said Topher. "A pirate's treasure!" exclaimed Mattie.

"Hi, Pax, Pili and Paisley! Look at my new locket! Isn't it gorgeous?" asked Ripley.

"Locket? What locket? We don't see any locket," said the three puzzled baby possums.

"Why, it's right around my neck. Where is it?
Oh NO! It's GONE!" yowled Ripley.

Ripley ran full speed into the house to find her brother Hariel.

"Help, Hariel! Help! My new locket is gone! What do I do?" cried a panicked Ripley.

Living as an upside-down goldfish gave Hariel a unique view of the world. He always had good advice.

"First, breathe slowly to calm yourself. Then, go find Pele. She is the best search and rescue dog around. If anyone knows what to do, it's our sister," said Hariel.

"Pele, I need your help! It's an emergency!" cried Ripley. "I've lost my new locket and I don't know what to do."

Pele thought for a moment, then offered her best solution: "First, you need to search high, low, inside, outside and all around."

"If you don't find it, then you must ask your friends to help because each of them has a special way of looking at the world. I can gather everyone together and help you organize a search."

"Don't worry, Ripley. We will find your locket," promised Pele.

Ripley thanked Pele and scampered off to the kitchen. She always began her day there, so it was a good place to start her search.

"First, I'll search high," decided Ripley. She made a quick jump up onto the kitchen counter and carefully climbed onto the top of the toaster oven.

Standing on her tippy toe beans, she reached up and pulled open the cabinet door. After much poking around, Ripley came up empty-pawed.

"It's not up high," she meowed with disappointment.

Next, Ripley raced downstairs. Earlier that day, she had played in a drawer with lots of crinkly wrapping paper and colorful ribbons. Ribbons were one of her favorite things.

"I've searched high. Now, I'll search low," thought Ripley. She flexed her little toe beans, gripped the knob and pulled until the drawer opened.

After carefully pawing through all the wrapping paper and ribbons, there was no locket to be found.

"It's not down low," she sighed sadly.

"Hey, Ripley! Pele said you needed help. Are you looking for these?" asked Kapo.

"Thanks Kapo, but those are tennis balls, not my locket," huffed Ripley.

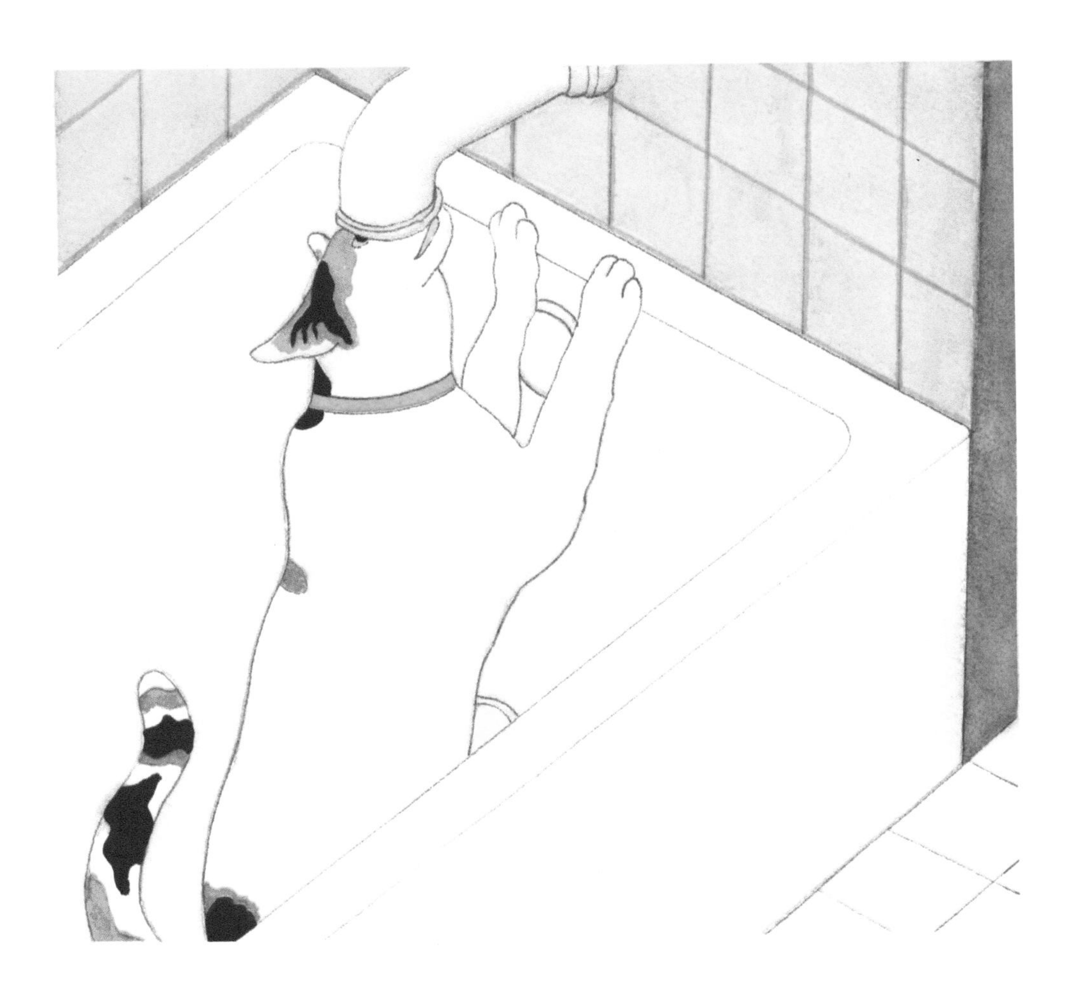

"Oh! I was in the bathroom this morning, admiring my locket in the mirror," remembered Ripley.

She rushed to the bathroom and searched every nook and cranny, even inside the bathtub waterspout. No locket.

"It's not inside," she howled hopelessly.

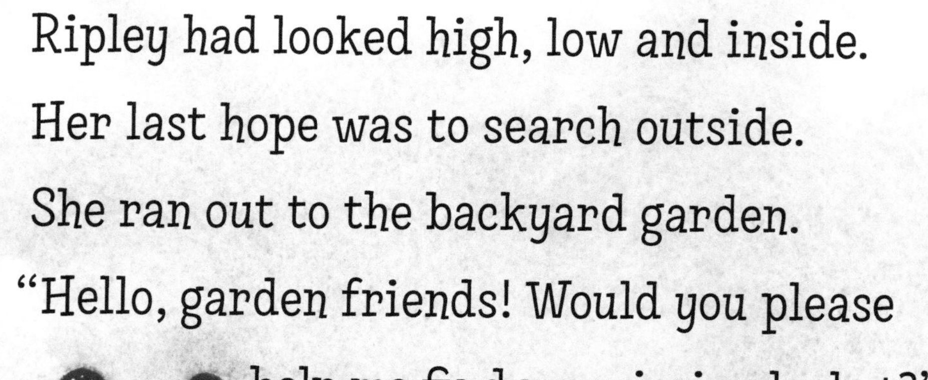

Ripley had looked high, low and inside.
Her last hope was to search outside.
She ran out to the backyard garden.
"Hello, garden friends! Would you please
help me find my missing locket?"
pleaded Ripley.

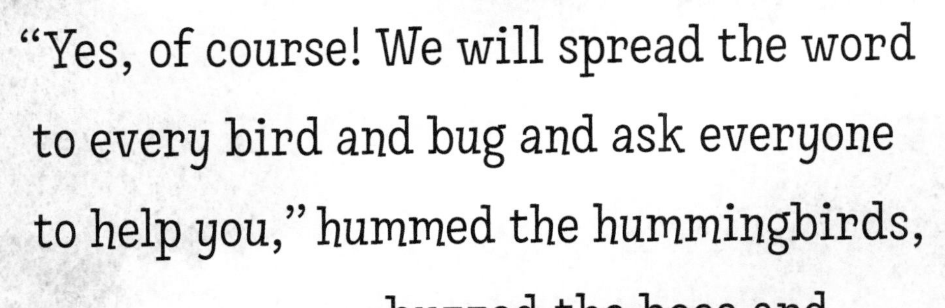

"Yes, of course! We will spread the word to every bird and bug and ask everyone to help you," hummed the hummingbirds,

buzzed the bees and fluttered the butterflies.

"Let's eat some nectar for energy, stretch our wings and fly to every flower. We will ask our flapping, flittering friends to search far and wide for Ripley's missing locket!" fluttered the butterflies.

"Bzzz, bzzz, bzzz! Time to form our Honeycomb Brigade! Ripley needs our help. Our mission: find her shiny new locket. Spread the word to every ladybug, cricket, beetle, fly and ant you meet!" buzzed the very busy bees.

Word spread fast among the hummingbirds
since they were fast at everything.
“Let’s all help Ripley find her locket.
Fly as quickly as you can, search the skies
and ask every bird you meet to look
for her locket!” hummed the hummers.

"Did you hear the news Topher? Ripley needs our help. I bet we'll be the first to find her locket. Let's go!" said Mattie.

Topher remembered a shiny thing he once saw in the tree hollow.

"I found it Mattie!" he yelled.

SAN FRANSISCO CHRONICLE
MISSING LOCKET

Mattie was busy digging through the recycling bin, or as she liked to call it, her "Pirate's Treasure Chest." She remembered seeing lots of shiny things in there.

There were tin cans, paper clips, a gold candy wrapper, two silver buttons, a bit of Christmas tree tinsel, a lightbulb, a tiny mirror and one very, very, shiny bottle cap.

"I found it, Topher!" Mattie yelled back.

As it turned out, Mattie and Topher both found shiny things, a bell for Topher and the bottle cap for Mattie. But unfortunately, neither shiny thing was Ripley's locket.

"It's up to me now!" thought Nash. "I will find Ripley's locket super-duper fast so we can go back to playing Touch Nose Tag."

"How about this yummy walnut? Who wouldn't want a tasty snack instead of a locket?"

“Or what about this peanut? Peanuts are much better than a silly locket!” exclaimed Nash.

“Hey, this acorn looks like a locket. An acorn dangles from a tree, just like a locket would dangle around Ripley’s neck.”

Nash had found three different nuts in record time, but the nuts were not particularly shiny and definitely not Ripley’s locket.

Mama P watched as Pax, Pili and Paisley carefully combed through all the plants and turned over every rock in the backyard.

“Mama P! Come look! We found the locket! We found the locket!” screamed the three baby possums.

“Good job, you three! Yes, you did find a locket,” said Mama P. “But unfortunately, that is not Ripley’s locket. It belongs to the two-legged creature who lives in the house. We will leave it on the porch for her to find.”

Mattie, Topher, Nash, Mama P and her three Ps had done their best to find Ripley’s locket in the backyard garden. It was definitely not there.

Time for a new plan.

"Good effort, everyone," said Pele.
"We now know that Ripley's locket is not in the house or backyard."

Ripley tried very hard not to cry. She was starting to feel like she'd never see her beautiful, shiny locket again.

Pele thought about all the times she had searched for missing humans. "We need to broaden our search area," she suggested.

"Based on information brought to us by the hummingbirds, our next search area is the Oakland Rose Garden. It will be a bit of a walk, so let's all drink some water and eat a snack. Then, we will head out."

The determined little search team and
their hummingbird guide marched
through the backyard and Bamboo Forest,
all the way to the Oakland Rose Garden.

“We made it! Now what do we do? How will we find my locket here?” asked Ripley.

“Let’s find someone and ask them for help. Look, here comes a very big turkey. They look like they’re in charge,” said Pele.

“Well, well, well...what have we here? I am The Mayor. Welcome to the Oakland Rose Garden. Would you like a tour?” gobbled the turkey as he shook his wattle and proudly spread his tail feathers.

“No thank you, Mayor. We are on a search mission for my sister’s missing locket. Our hummingbird friends told us we might find it here,” answered Pele.

"Check our Lost and Found. It is under the roof eaves by that window," said The Mayor. "Ring the bell, and Mango the Magpie will come to meet you."

Nash scampered up the tree and beat Mattie and Topher to the bell. He grabbed the bell and shook it hard. Ring-a-ding, ring-a-ding, ring-a-ding!

LOST'N'FOUND

Mango the Magpie did not get many visitors to her Lost and Found. She quickly hopped down to see who was ringing the bell.

"Hello! Are you Mango?" asked Nash. "The Mayor sent us. We are looking for my friend's missing locket."

"Yes, that's me! Is your friend's locket shiny? Because I have found many shiny things. Let's look through my Lost and Found together," said Mango.

Nash and Mango looked and looked. Nash was losing hope. Suddenly, Mango held up a sparkly locket!

RIPLEY
CRAYOLA
THE ACME THUNDERER
CENTS

"Is this Ripley's locket?" asked Mango.

"Yes! Yes it is! Oh, my goodness.
We found it!" exclaimed Nash.
"Ripley is going to be so happy."

Nash quickly scampered down from the Lost and Found, carefully holding onto Ripley's locket. "Ripley! We found it! yelled Nash.

Ripley ran up to Nash with the biggest smile on her face. "My locket! Oh, thank you, thank you!" she happily meowed.

Nash proudly handed Ripley her locket. "Let's go home and celebrate," he said with a smile.

The search for Ripley's missing locket was a success! After thanking Mango and The Mayor, everyone happily made their way home together, chattering away about their big adventure.

Only Ripley was quiet as the little search team walked home. Lots of thoughts swirled around inside her head, like puffs of fog on a gray, cloudy day.

"I felt beautiful when I admired my locket in the mirror," she mused.

"And when I showed my locket to everyone, I felt proud and important."

"After I lost the locket, I felt upset and desperate to find it."

"But even when I felt so low, searching with everyone was the best adventure ever, better than actually finding my locket."

RIPLEY

RIPLEY

Suddenly, Ripley had an "Aha!" moment. It was as if the sun had come out and cleared away all the gray clouds.

"A locket is just a pretty thing. Not special like my family and friends," she excitedly realized.

"I want to celebrate them! They are wonderful and more precious to me than a gazillion shiny lockets!"

It had been a long day, and their big locket finding adventure was finally over. Home never looked so good. Ripley was in high spirits and ready to celebrate.

Ripley climbed up everyone's favorite tree and licked her tired toe beans. She noticed that each toe bean was just a little different from the other.

"That's it! There is something different about each one of my family and friends," exclaimed Ripley.

"Hariel gives good advice. Kapo is full of energy. Pele is a good leader."

"Nash never gives up. Pax, Pili and Paisley are good diggers. Mattie and Topher love adventure."

"Everyone used their special talents to help me," thought Ripley with amazement.

An idea suddenly popped into Ripley's head. She carefully climbed down the tree and zipped inside the house.

Ripley ran straight to her napping place where her favorite toys were waiting.

"Hello, my babies! We are back from our search adventure and I am happy to report that we found my missing locket!" purred Ripley.

"I have a favor to ask of you. May I leave my locket with you? That way, I know it will always be safe and never get lost again."

Ripley carefully placed the locket with her babies. She knew they would take very good care of it.

Ripley gave each baby a lick and a kiss. Then, she scampered off to find her two-legged family.

RIPLEY

Ripley found her two-legged Mama cooking dinner in the kitchen.

"Mama, can you help me?" she meowed. "I want to surprise everyone with a special celebration party."

"Of course, little one. I have a very good idea what everyone will love. Let's have your party after dinner," said Mama.

Ripley happily purred, stretched and rubbed her little face on Mama's legs. "Thank you, Mama! You're the best!" trilled Ripley.

VANILLA
VANILLA
POPS
POPS
FRUIT
VEGGIE
POPS

"Surprise! It's ICE CREAM PARTY time!" squealed Ripley.

"Hooray for ice cream!" shouted everyone. Suddenly, it got very quiet as they all happily ate their icy treats.

Every day brings us moments to love
and cherish our family and friends,
dear reader.

Ripley will be waiting for you to join
her for more adventures, more laughter
and more fun!

But first, we must clean the ice cream
off our paws and faces!

(Not) The End

Here's a Sneak Peek at Ripley's next exciting adventure: Ripley's Road Trip.

Ripley, Pele, Kapo and their two-legged family hit the open road! Have fun traveling with them up the Pacific Coast, from the San Francisco Bay Area to Vancouver, British Colombia. Dip your toe beans in the big blue ocean and make lots of new splashing, hopping, burrowing friends along the way!

Ripley had never seen the ocean or anything like it. The sun shone bright, covering the waves with a blanket of sparkly silver glitter. She could not stop looking at it.

"The ocean is so beautiful. Does Hariel know there is this much water to swim in?" Ripley wondered.

A Message from Ripley's Two-legged Family

After reading Ripley's Missing Locket, you now know that Ripley, her family and friends find her locket in Mango's Lost and Found at the Oakland Rose Garden.

The inspiration for the rose garden illustrations comes from the real-life Morcom Rose Garden, a public jewel that spans more than seven acres. Named after the Oakland mayor who planted the first rose in 1932, the formal garden is surrounded by a ramble of winding paths, graceful stairways and dramatic water features. It also attracts and provides sanctuary for a variety of birds and other creatures, including turkeys—and one in particular who thinks he runs the place.

We walk at the rose garden several times a week and are always grateful for the Friends of the Morcom Rose Garden, an amazing volunteer group. Its members help the wonderful gardeners from the City of Oakland tend to the roses and keep the garden looking breathtakingly beautiful year-round. Our heartfelt thanks to all who care for this incredible place.

It is so much fun to share Ripley's stories with you, and to have you be a part of our Bamboo Forest community. Kapo sends a warm woof your way!

– CONNIE & MARK HERRICK

Lightning Source UK Ltd.
Milton Keynes UK
UKHW050613160223
417099UK00018B/279